THE RED BALL

by JOANNA YARDLEY

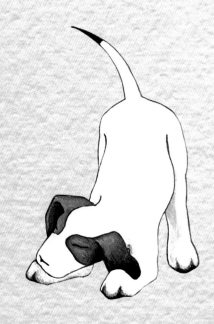

JANE YOLEN BOOKS

HARCOURT BRACE JOVANOVICH, PUBLISHERS

San Diego   New York   London

Requests for permission to make copies of
any part of the work should be mailed to:
Permissions Department,
Harcourt Brace Jovanovich, Publishers,
Orlando, Florida 32887.

Library of Congress Cataloging-in-Publication Data
Yardley, Joanna.
The red ball / written and illustrated by Joanna Yardley. — 1st ed.
p.   cm.
"Jane Yolen books."
Summary: A little girl searching for her red ball
finds it in a photograph and as she pursues it,
it moves to other photographs depicting a girl
very much like herself.
ISBN 0-15-200894-2
[1. Family — Fiction. 2. Balls (Sporting goods) — Fiction.]
I. Title.
PZ7.Y1958Re   1991
[E] — dc19   88-26794

Printed in Singapore
B C D E

To Mom and Dad

JOHN AND VALERIE YARDLEY

On the day Max snatched Joanie's favorite red ball,

he bounded away

up the attic stairs.

Joanie followed him

into a room full of shadows.

She could just see his tail

beneath the mirror.

She yanked.

He jumped.

Over went a box

of old photographs.

But where was her red ball?

Joanie picked up

one of the photos

and stared.

There was the red ball

in the hands of a baby

in a large carriage.

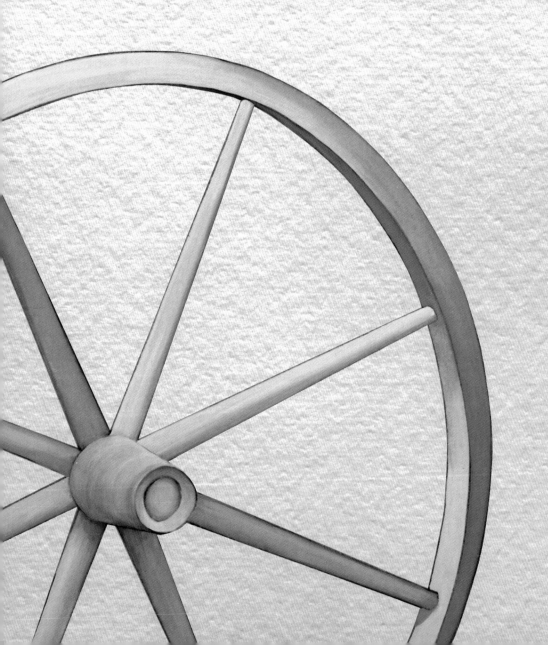

"That's *my* ball,"

Joanie whispered.

But just as Joanie

reached for it,

the baby tossed

the ball away.

Joanie picked up

another photograph

where against a long seacoast

a little girl played croquet

with the red ball.

"My ball!" Joanie cried,

bending over to pick it up.

But before she could,

the little girl knocked the ball away.

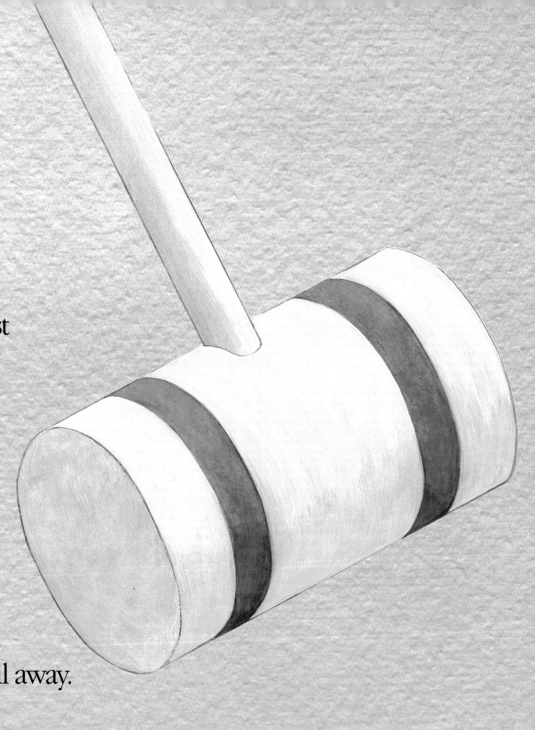

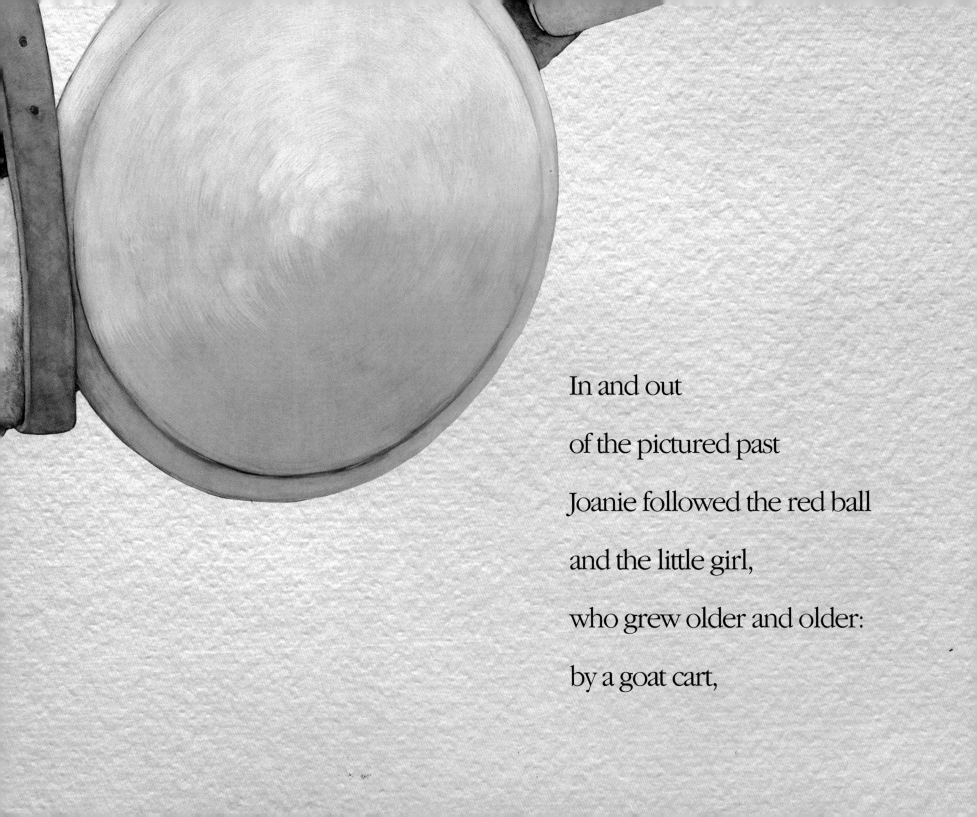

In and out

of the pictured past

Joanie followed the red ball

and the little girl,

who grew older and older:

by a goat cart,

ALLEN S HILL

into a fine house,

off to school,

even to a pottery

where the girl now worked.

But Joanie was never

quite quick enough

to get back her red ball.

At last Joanie sat down

next to the woman

who had the red ball

in the middle of her lap

and a baby by her side.

They didn't even notice

how tired Joanie was.

She was almost too tired to pick up

the last photograph. But when she did,

she saw her own mother holding a little baby.

And there was the girl Joanie had been following

through all the pictured years, only now

she had white hair. Joanie knew her

because she still held the red ball.

Clutching the photograph

Joanie jumped

down the stairs.

Max followed.

Dropping into her mother's lap,

Joanie showed her the picture.

"Why, Joanie," her mother said,

"it's an old photo of us.

That's you as a baby.

And that's Grandma Robinson

on the day she gave you

her favorite red ball."

The illustrations in this book were done in gouache, Prismacolor, and Ticonderoga #2 pencils on sepia prints of original drawings made on tracing paper.

The display type was set in Americana.

The text type was set in ITC Garamond Light.

Composition by Thompson Type, San Diego, California

Printed and bound by Tien Wah Press, Singapore

Production supervision by Warren Wallerstein and Michele Green

Designed by Michael Farmer and Joy Chu